Thank you for choosing this coloring book!
Before you dive into your coloring adventure, please take a moment to read these tips:

Paper Quality:
Amazon's paper works beautifully with colored pencils and alcohol-based markers. To keep your artwork neat and avoid any color bleeding onto the next page, simply place a blank, thicker sheet of paper behind the page you're working on.
Enjoy!

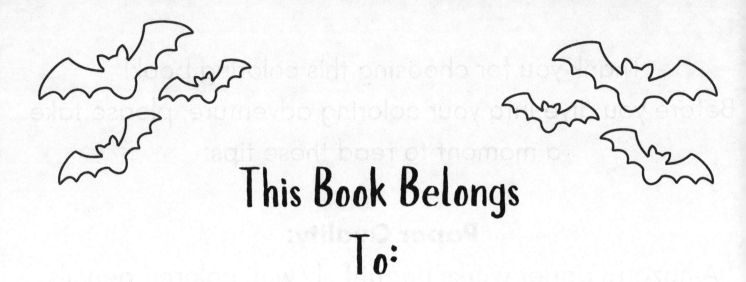

This Book Belongs
To:

_____

Color Test Page

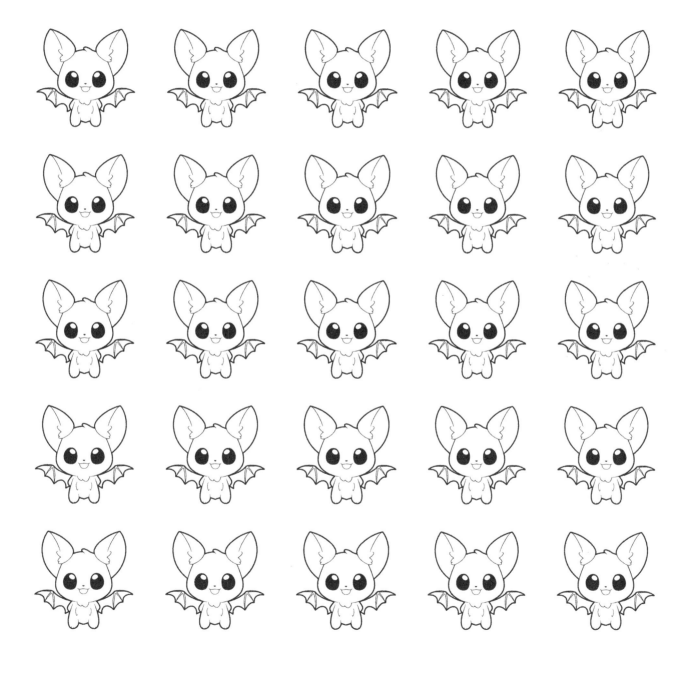

Your feedback is greatly appreciated!

Your feedback is invaluable to us in our mission to create the best books possible. By sharing your honest thoughts, you not only help us improve but also guide others in finding the right book for them.

We would deeply appreciate it if you could take just 60 seconds to leave a review on Amazon or the platform where you purchased the book. Your insights help other readers make informed decisions, and your support empowers us to continue delivering quality content.

To leave a review, simply find the book on the site where you purchased it, select a star rating, and share a few sentences about your experience.

Thank you for helping us grow and for guiding others in their coloring journey!

Review this product

Share your thoughts with other customers

Write a customer review

Made in the USA
Monee, IL
29 November 2024

71655395R00057